BUSY, BUSY MOUSE

by VIRGINIA KROLL

illustrated by FUMI KOSAKA

SCHOLASTIC INC.

New York Toronto London Auckland Sydney
Mexico City New Delhi Hong Kong Buenos Aires

ISBN 0-439-64425-9

Text copyright © 2003 by Virginia Kroll. Illustrations copyright © 2003 by Fumi Kosaka. All rights reserved. Published by Scholastic Inc., 557 Broadway, New York, NY 10012, by arrangement with Viking Children's Books, a member of Penguin Group (USA) Inc. SCHOLASTIC and associated logos are trademarks and/or registered trademarks of Scholastic Inc.

12 11 10 9 8 7 6 5 4 3 2 1   4 5 6 7 8 9/0

Printed in the U.S.A.   40

First Scholastic printing, February 2004

Set in Clarendon
Book design by Teresa Kietlinski

With love to Father Walter Szczesny,
my busy, busy friend.

– V.K.

To Kyushu no Obachan,
who has always been there for me
and my family despite her busy life!

– F. K.

Up comes the sun.
Good morning, everyone.

Baby crying.
Eggs frying.

Clay smashing.
Blocks bashing.

Telephone ringing.
Canary singing.

Pictures scribbled.
Cookies nibbled.

All the day,
Eat, talk, play.

Busy, busy house . . .

Quiet, quiet mouse.

Down goes the sun.
Good evening, everyone.

Clay put back.
Blocks in a stack.

Canary fed.
Stories read.

Teeth brushed.
Baby hushed.

Off to bed,
You sleepyhead.

All the night,
Sleeping tight.
Quiet, quiet house . . .

Busy, busy mouse!